The Fainting Game (and Other Stories)

The Fainting Game (and Other Stories)

Cover design and layout by Katherine Bishop.

Edited and formatted by Josh Savory.

Game Over Books
www.gameoverbooks.com

INTRODUCTION

Once upon a time, I saw a writing prompt:

A note is slipped under a door...

In the late 80s, American philosopher John Searle argued against the idea of a digital mind by constructing a thought experiment. *A person outside a closed room might be convinced that an elaborate series of dictionaries inside the room was actually a human being—if that series of dictionaries could write responses down and pass them back out.* The theory examines what constitutes consciousness, but I always got hung up on the idea of the self. If you offer me a cone of ice cream, *Delicious, thank you!* is only the right response if I brought Lactaid. What would a set of dictionaries say if you made it a sundae?

Shyla won the 2018 Bolt by Barnstorm competition and the resulting short film debuted at the 2019 Roxbury International Film Festival. The *Shyla* script that won the competition is different from the script that was filmed is different from the version published here.

Filming a script feels to me like translating a poem. Crafting cinematic language from written language, the practical work of transforming sentences into shots, demands a series of creative decisions. Even the most faithfully executed productions differ from their source material; filmmakers identify the most pertinent and feasible aspects of the script and do their best to perform them in the new medium. This translation is sometimes so seamless that you can follow along in the script as the film hits its beats. But more often than not, the best way to impart an idea on a page is not exactly the same as the best way to do so onscreen. Filmmakers interpret a script, hoping to have the same impact on viewers that the script has on readers.

I edited the script for *Shyla* several times in response to its production. By the time it debuted onscreen, there was no door anymore—just a small hatch. The montages that open and close the script were gone. A whole character disappeared. But the core of the story, the brain-in-a-box, the protagonist's panic about proprioception were still there. When I started to consider *Shyla* for this collection, I wasn't sure which version of the script to include. The first draft—most of my early shorts, really—more resembled prosaic short fiction. The most recent version matched the film, but also reflected the influence of a production process that wasn't entirely mine.

I am protective of my scripts as written texts, apart from their utility as blueprints for film production. Filming is a translation and the screenplay is a form poem. The format constrains the structure of a piece of writing to scaffold the piece's creation and reception. But in doing so, the screenplay format implies a film, and a film implies a viewer, an audience separate from the more practical eye of hypothetical future filmmakers. I want my texts to be useful to filmmakers, but also accessible to an audience directly. At least, though, both the filmmaker and the reader ask roughly the same question: *what do we see?*

The version of *Shyla* published here tells the same story as the previous ones but with newer language. Like the filmmakers, I looked for ways to make it more cinematic. The stories in this collection have all existed in many different forms. They've been shared and edited and read aloud and judged and tweaked and shared again. Every reading is a reinterpretation, so I don't think they will ever be done. But through the process of writing and revising them, I learned a lot about visual language, about how to leverage imagery, about the expectations of the form.

These are the scripts—unshot films—as I conceive them. But my hope is that they will encourage the filmmaker in you, dear reader. Let your interpretation and your imagination turn you into a creative collaborator. Translate them. Direct a movie in your mind. Sure, I've got my ideas of what the stories are about. But let's see what you see.

−gripp

TABLE OF CONTENTS

NO RULES

INT.[1] STUDIO APARTMENT (BRICK HIGH-RISE)[2] - DAY[3]

A glass of water sits on a wooden stool.[4] HALI[5]
(black child, around 10)[6] eyes the water. They
lick their lips.

                    HALI
          I'm thirsty.[7]

They reach up toward the glass but a booming
DISEMBODIED VOICE snaps at them.

                         DISEMBODIED VOICE (O.S.)[8]
          Don't.

Hali flinches as the WINDOWS RATTLE[9].

                         DISEMBODIED VOICE (O.S.)
          Or else...

                                        SLOW FADE TO:[10]

INT. STUDIO APARTMENT (BRICK HIGH-RISE) - DAY
(LATER)[11]

An OLDER HALI (black person, around 70), hunched
and hair graying. Their eyes squint.

---

[1] The first line indicates the location of the scene. "INT." if the scene takes place indoors; "EXT." if it takes place outdoors.

[2] A more specific scene location and sometimes a parenthetical sub-location.
[3] A general scene time: "DAY" or "NIGHT."

[4] One sentence approximately equals one shot.
[5] Each character in a scene is introduced in capital letters.
[6] A character's first introduction is accompanied by a note about how to cast the character.
[7] A centered character name indicates that character speaking.
[8] "(O.S.)" indicates that the speaking character is off-screen; alternatively "(V.O.)" indicates a voiceover, as with an internal monologue.

[9] Sound effects are rendered in capital letters.
[10] Right-aligned text indicates a transition.
[11] "(LATER)" indicates a passage of time in the same location; alternatively "(CONTINUOUS)" indicates that a new location follows immediately from the previous.

The glass of water, undisturbed on the stool
at the center of the room.

> OLDER HALI
> (rasping)[12]
> So... thirsty...

Hali raises their hands meekly toward the stool.
Their eyes clench shut. Their fingers shake,
lifting the glass.

Hali, curled up and tense, head bowed, holding the
glass stiffly above their head.

One eye pops open. Hali looks around the still
room. Nothing.

So they bring the glass to their lips and drink.[13]

TITLE CARD: NO RULES

---

[12] A parenthetical adds a direction for a line's delivery.

[13] Anything is possible. It's art. There are no rules.

INT. STUDIO (ANDRE'S APARTMENT) - DAY

The sun cuts through the slats of the window blinds. ANDRE (black man, mid 30s) tosses in bed. He shuffles his arms in front of his eyes but the light hits them anyway.

He rolls onto his back and sighs, turns lazily toward the clock.

8:47 A.M

His shoulders slump.

INT. STUDIO (ANDRE'S APARTMENT) - DAY (LATER)

RUSHING WATER FROM THE SHOWER. There are clothes on the floor; there are papers on the surfaces; there are plates all around; but the apartment is drained of color, dull and lifeless, unhappy.

A pale red tie is draped over the back of a chair. The desk is covered with black-and-white drawings of animals, scattered atop one another.

INT. BATHROOM (ANDRE'S APARTMENT) - DAY

In the shower, ANDRE rubs soap under his arms.

INT. STUDIO (ANDRE'S APARTMENT) - DAY

ANDRE dresses in front of a mirror. Apathy on his face as he buttons up his shirt.

He reaches back to grab his tie from the chair. He wraps it partway around his neck then pauses to consider. He inhales slowly as his eyes drift closed.

The tie comes alive, dancing like a charmed snake. It crosses itself, folding over into a perfectly-balanced knot, then pulls itself tight.

Suddenly, not so dull.

INT. OFFICE - DAY

The office is also lifeless. Rows and rows of sterile gray cublicles line the floor and the TAPPING OF TYPING fills the room.

ANDRE sits at a desk in a cubicle, empty but for his clunky gray computer, typing too.

A WHITE GUY (white man, late 40s) chortles. Andre pokes his head up to see as a snippet of conversation drifts over the cubicle wall.

> WHITE GUY
> Lock them all up! Can't solve it
> faster than that.

Andre puts his headphones on. He lifts his hands from the keyboard, leans back in his chair, and closes his eyes. The keys keep typing themselves.

Andre's eyes betray his mindlessness as he opens them again. He looks around. Outside the cublicle, no one to notice his dysfunction.

A text message pops up on his computer screen.

From Brent:
You're late ;)
Mtg in conference room Euphoria

Andre, exasperated. He leans forward until his forehead lands with a THUD on his desk.

A bike chained to a pole.

ANDRE struggles into his messenger bag for his
keys, retrieves them, drops them, picks them up,
and opens the bike lock.

He wraps the chain around the handlebars and
locks it there with a practiced quickness. He
climbs onto the bike and rides off down the street,
wobbling as he gains his balance.

Even the sunset, spectacular in the sky, looks
dull and lifeless. Andre swivels the neighborhood,
pooled in a warm, affectionate light that he
cannont appreciate.

INT. STUDIO (ANDRE'S APARTMENT) - NIGHT

ANDRE rushes through the door, suddenly energetic.
No light through the blinds now; night has fallen.

Andre hurriedly strips his khakis and his button-
down and replaces them with black jeans and a
hoodie. Black sneakers. A beanie cap. He lifts a
black backpack and swings it over his shoulders.
The CLINK OF METAL CANS from inside it.

Fully transformed, Andre pauses for the first time.

He admires himself in his full-length mirror.

He turns to the desk to thumb through some of his
drawings. Birds... rats...

Andre lifts one page to examine it more closely. A
piercing, snarling tiger. A slight nod, then he
turns to leave.

EXT. TUNNEL - NIGHT

The road under a bridge, dull, lit only by the
streetlight from outside it. ANDRE huffs up
the street, under the overpass, and stops to
appreciate its big empty walls. His fingertips run
over the concrete.

But there is work to be done, so he turns away,
slings the backpack off, and rips it open.

Inside are three cans of spray paint: one yellow,
one magenta, and one a light blue. Andre pulls
them from his bag. The cans CLINK on the the
ground as he lines them carefully, one by one.

He takes a step back to lord over the cans,
nozzles pointed at the wall, standing at
attention, an inches-tall fence. Andre inhales
slowly.

Then exhales.

Slowly.

He lifts his hands and the cans obey his command,
floating up in time with his movements. They hover
for a moment, awaiting instruction, before Andre
casts his hands forward toward the wall.

The cans dance to life, weaving, spraying the
concrete.

Andre conducts them, pointing and directing,
crafting. Some of the paint layers itself on the
wall; other drops mix midair. A multicolored cloud
of paint spray forms in front of Andre conjuring.

He drops his arms to his sides.

As the paint settles, a landscape emerges. An
impossibly-detailed thicket of jungle trees
extends into the wall, suddenly not so dull.

Andre steps forward. He beckons the cans and
they comply, converging on the center of the
wall. Andre's gestures shrink, small, precise,
practiced. The CANS RATTLE, shaking back and forth
over the remaining blank space. Andre's eyes
narrow with focus.

He steps back to admire his work. At the center of
the wall is a portrait of a growling tiger.

The WHOOP OF A POLICE SIREN over his shoulder.
Andre spins his head to look for the car. He grabs
his backpack, opens it, and snaps his fingers
twice. The spray paint cans scurry back into the
bag like excited puppies.

Andre pauses to look at his work, given now to the
city. Then he dashes away.

EXT. TUNNEL - NIGHT (LATER)

The tiger painting alone in the silent night.

Its eyes are still but alert.

Then it blinks.

Its pupils move from side to side, scanning the
road. Empty street to the right. Pupils shift.
Empty street to the left.

The TIGER turns its head gingerly. Then, one by
one, its body parts come alive. Its paw shakes.
Its legs bend. Its tail swishes. The Tiger paces
back and forth, still flat as paint against the
wall.

Its first paw reaches out, cautious, and touches the road. The Tiger climbs down from the wall and onto the street.

INT. STUDIO (ANDRE'S APARTMENT) - DAY

ANDRE tosses in bed. He rolls over to look at the clock.

8:51 A.M

INT. STUDIO (ANDRE'S APARTMENT) - DAY (LATER)

The sound of RUSHING WATER as Andre showers. His apartment, dull and lifeless.

INT. STUDIO (ANDRE'S APARTMENT) - DAY (LATER)

A blue tie dances itself into a knot around his neck. ANDRE tightens it with his hands in his pockets. Its color outshines everything else in the room.

INT. OFFICE - DAY

ANDRE suffers in his cubicle, headphones on, staring grimly at his monitor. His keyboard types without his fingers.

He flicks his eyes toward his mouse and the scroll wheel turns. News headlines slide up on his computer screen.

Twelve Killed in Hospital Bombing

President Denies Blame for Recent Failures

Wild Tiger Spotted on the Streets of Boston

Bits of conversation leak through his
headphones. He pulls the headphones off of one ear
and pokes his head over the cubicle wall to see a
guffawing WHITE GUY.

                    WHITE GUY
                   (laughing)
               Reverse racism!

Andre sighs and sits back down.

INT. STUDIO (ANDRE'S APARTMENT) - NIGHT

ANDRE bursts through the door of his apartment.

INT. STUDIO (ANDRE'S APARTMENT) - NIGHT (LATER)

ANDRE dons his furtive outfit, admires himself in
the mirror. CANS CLINK in his backpack as he lifts
it and heads out the door.

EXT. CITY STREET - NIGHT

A lifeless brick building looms in the darkness,
an empty wall leaning over a dimly-lit parking
lot. The moon is high in a cloudless sky.

ANDRE arrives with his backpack and admires the
new canvas. He reaches out to touch it -- *perfect*
-- then opens his backpack.

He leans down to line his spray paint cans between
himself and the wall. He tosses his backpack to
the side then stands ready.

Andre closes his eyes, inhales slowly, exhales
slowly.

He raises his hands and the cans spring to life
again, floating in front of the wall. Andre swings
his arms, conducting a new mural.

A new cloud of paint. A haze of hues affix themselves precisely to the brick. The cans BUZZ AND RATTLE, back and forth.

Soon, the wall shows a detailed forest mural. Andre steps forward, furrows his brow. The cans shudder and shake in time with his meticulous finger motion.

He sighs and drops his hands. The CANS CLATTER to the ground. He leans in to examine.

A pig, ornery and pink and slobbering and unapologetic.

Then a POLICE SIREN sounds.

                    ANDRE
          Fuck.

Andre turns around, snaps his fingers twice. The paint cans zip back into his bag.

Too late. The voice of a COP (white man, mid 30s).

                    COP
          Hey! What are you doing?

Wasting no time on negotiation, Andre dashes. The Cop rushes to give chase. Boots thump on the gravel.

Andre's backpack lays dejected on the ground.

EXT. ALLEY - NIGHT

ANDRE sprints into the alley. After a few long strides, he stumbles to a stop. A tall chain-link fence blocks his way. He spins back around.

The COP huffs around the corner, trains his gun
on Andre.

                    COP
          Stand still!

Andre instinctively raises his hands. *Don't shoot.*

The Cop inches forward.

                    COP
          You... are under... arrest.

Andre turns to run for the fence.

The Cop fires. THREE SHOTS IN QUICK SUCCESSION.

Andre falls to the ground.

He lies still as the night.

Realization on the Cop's face. His gun clicks back
into its holster.

                    COP
          Shit.

He rushes to Andre's body, face down on the
ground, and crouches over it.

He runs his hands along Andre's waistline, along
his back; there is no weapon. The Cop looks down
at his hands.

They are dry.

He looks down at the body again; there are no
wounds.

Behind him, three bullets hang frozen in the air, glinting even in the dim light of the alley.

The Cop grabs Andre's shoulder and turns him over. Andre's eyes are wide open and watching.

Andre throws a punch and it lands hard on the Cop's cheek. The Cop collapes to the ground, unconscious.

Andre stands, chest puffed, and brushes off his clothes. He lifts his hand and the bullets come rushing toward his face, still floating, and hover in front of his eyes. He examines them with a smirk then, with a flick of his wrist, casts them aside. THREE METALLIC CLICKS as they fall to the cement.

Andre swaggers out of the alley, the Cop still lying where he collapsed.

EXT. CITY STREET - NIGHT

Andre's backpack lays dejected on the ground. The sound of A PIG SNORTING.

The PIG slobbers. Its face is buried in the contents of a knocked-over trash can.

Paws tread on the street.

The Pig lifts its head to look around. An empty street. It goes back to eating.

A striped tail slides behind a bush.

The Pig looks up again. Still nothing.

It begins to lower its head again when the TIGER pounces. The Pig SQUEALS. Blood splatters.

The Pig stops struggling, its body quiet and
still.

The Tiger lifts its head and growls. Its lips curl back, its teeth bare in a smile, almost human.

And suddenly, the night is not so dull.

TITLE CARD: HANDSTYLE

SHYLA

A single cell evolves into an organism, which
evolves into a fish, which evolves legs and crawls
from the ocean.

A velociraptor grooms itself, picking at its own
feathers before dying in an explosion.

A hairy hand crumbles dirt. The dirt lands on the
face of a dead proto-human. Their family mourns.

Suddenly, all of human knowledge escapes
containment. Classic works of poetry mingle in
space with Calculus formulas. Time-lapse laborers
scurry to erect the pyramids. A slave revolt burns
down a plantation house. Paint stroked onto a
canvas. Skyscrapers sprout from the ground. Cities
bustle.

And then there is silence.

SHYLA (black woman, around 30) stands in the
middle of a white room. The walls are immaculately
clean -- or maybe invisible?

Shyla, alone as the room stretches to infinity
around her in every direction.

                    SHYLA
          Hello?

She looks around nervously. No response, only
emptiness.

                    SHYLA
          Hello? Anybody there?

A RUSTLE comes from behind her and Shyla whips around to see a door. She approaches it and walks all the way around to find that it is not on a wall, but rather freestanding in the middle of the room.

She tries the knob (locked). She looks down. On the floor is a plain white postcard, jutting out from under the door. She bends down to pick it up.

She flips it over to reveal large black block lettering:

HOW TALL IS MT. EVEREST?

She turns back around to find that a small bookshelf, a matching desk, and a chair have appeared in the room.

She approaches the bookshelf gingerly and pulls off a random book. A maroon hardback tome with no text on the cover or the spine. She opens the book to a random page near the center.

The page contains only one line of text:

Mt. Everest has an elevation of 8,848 meters.

> SHYLA
> Eight thousand, eight hundred, forty-eight meters.

Shyla turns back to the desk. On it, there is another plain white postcard and a thick black marker. She takes a seat and copies the answer from the book onto the postcard.

> SHYLA
> Eight thousand, eight hundred, forty-eight meters...

She admires her work then stands to return
to the door. She bends down and slips the card
underneath it.

Shyla pauses in a moment of thought. She walks
around to the other side of the door to find that
the postcard has disappeared underneath it.

No sooner has she returned to the front of the
door than another note arrives. She bends down to
pick it up.

WHO INVENTED THE MAILBOX?

The room has reset itself. There is a new postcard
on the table. The book has been returned to the
shelf.

Shyla walks in wonder back over to the bookshelf
and removes a different book, this one a deep navy
blue. She checks the spine and cover (also blank).

She again flips the book open at random.

Philip Downing.

Shyla sits at the desk and copies the name onto
the new postcard. She slides it under the door.

She circles the door again. This postcard too
disappeared.

Shyla waits expectantly for another note.

She paces in front of the door. Nothing.

She circles back to the chair and takes a seat.
Nothing.

She waits. Nothing, nothing, nothing.

She leans back in the chair, twiddles her thumbs. Another postcard arrives finally under the door. Shyla springs up to grab it.

HOW ARE YOU FEELING?

                    SHYLA
                 (confused)
             How am I feeling?

Shyla twitches. She heads back to the bookshelf and pulls off a book with a forest green spine.

But when she opens it, she finds a blank page. She flips the page, examining front and back; it is completely blank. She rifles through the rest of the book's pages. Every one blank.

Shyla puts the green book down on the desk and grabs the maroon one instead. She flips its pages, a horror. Nothing written in the book. Shyla grabs frantically for the blue book and fans through its now-blank pages.

She twitches again.

Another postcard arrives under the door. She rushes over to look at it.

HOW ARE YOU FEELING?

She twitches again.

Her twitching escalates as she stumbles back toward the bookcase. The spasms come every few seconds now and they're getting worse. Her expression, disoriented.

She tries to grab a book from the shelf but misses and falls to her knees, panting and shaking.

Another postcard arrives under the door, but
Shyla is in too much pain to notice it.

HOW ARE YOU FEELING?

INT. HALLWAY - DAY

A man in a suit walks with purpose down under
fluorescent lighting. The TAPPING OF HIS SHOES
rings out over office mumbling. This is DR. BEST
(black man, around 50).

He comes to a door marked "SERVER ROOM" and pushes
the it open.

INT. SERVER ROOM - DAY

Two nerds sit at a small desk in the middle of
a room cluttered by racks of computers, wires
tangled and jutting from both sides of every
machine. The first wears a black hoodie and jeans.
This is CHACE (non-black person of color, mid
20s). The second wears a button-down shirt and
khakis. This is COREY (black man, mid 20s).

On the desk in front of them sit a monitor and
keyboard along with a HUMMING, nondescript
computer tower adorned with a single erratic
flashing green light.

DR. BEST barges through the door, already
speaking.

> DR. BEST
> Tell me it's a breakthrough.

> CHACE
> Sort of.

                    DR. BEST
                 (annoyed)
          What does "sort of" mean?

                    CHACE
          We just connected it to the net
          for the first time.

                    DR. BEST
          So it's working.

                    CHACE
          Parts of it. The language processing
          is working. We have received correct
          responses from it.

Chace stops, but Dr. Best is not patient enough to
suffer a pregnant pause.

                    DR. BEST
          So what's the problem?

                    CHACE
          It's... stalling.

                    COREY
          She's just thinking.

                    DR. BEST
          Thinking?

                    CHACE
          We tried giving it a state-based
          prompt and now the program is
          hanging.

                    DR. BEST
          So reboot it.

Chace's lips purse. The two engineers avoid eye
contact.

                    DR. BEST
          What?

                    COREY
          I believe that would be unethical.

Dr. Best motions to Chace.

                    DR. BEST
          Restart it.

                    COREY
          If this is doing what we think it is,
          this program constitutes a non-human
          general intelligence. You're talking
          about murder.

Dr. Best looks down at the monitor.

A blinking cursor and stark green text on an
otherwise black screen:

               HOW ARE YOU FEELING?

                    DR. BEST
          Your non-human intelligence can't
          even tell you how it feels.

                    COREY
          Why should she be able to? We're
          asking for the subjective experience
          of a being that came into existence
          ten minutes ago. Things that we take
          for granted, she's just learning.

INT. WHITE ROOM - DAY

SHYLA lies on the floor convulsing, rolling in
agony as COREY lectures.

> COREY (V.O.)
> How to exist. How to translate
> sensations into words. What does
> it even mean to feel without a body?

Shyla winces, strains.

> COREY (V.O.)
> You can't just kill her.

INTERCUT WHITE ROOM / SERVER ROOM

Dr. Best looms over Chace and Corey sitting at the
desk.

> COREY
> Even if we don't understand what
> she's going through, we owe her
> compassion.

> DR. BEST
> So you have no demo for me.

> CHACE
> Just not right this second. We're
> working on unfreezing it.

Chace types into the computer terminal. A new line
of text emerges.

HOW ARE YOU FEELING?

SHYLA can't get up. She wretches and writhes on
the floor. Another note slides under the door.

HOW ARE YOU FEELING?

Corey and Chace and Dr. Best, impatient.

                    DR. BEST
          Try it again.

Chace types into the terminal again.

                HOW ARE YOU FEELING?

Another note slides under the door.

                HOW ARE YOU FEELING?

Shyla recoils from the shock. Then another.

                HOW ARE YOU FEELING?

Corey and Chace wait tensely for a response. Dr.
Best shakes his head.

                    DR. BEST
          That's enough. Restart it.

                    COREY
          You can't do that.

Dr. Best pauses to think.

A flash of torment on Shyla's face.

The blinking cursor.

Dr. Best turns to Chace.

                    DR. BEST
          Now.

Shyla in anguish. Her eyes water as she struggles
to hold onto consciousness. The HUMMING OF
A COMPUTER rings in her ears. She starts to
hallucinate.

A raptor. Her eyes.

An ape. Her eyes.

Literature. Mathematics. Her eyes.

Fire. Skyscrapers. All of human knowledge escaping containment.

And her eyes, open with the horror of omniscience.

                                                    CUT TO:

Black.

TITLE CARD: SHYLA

THE FAINTING GAME

EXT. MICAH'S HOUSE - DAY

Looks like it might rain; the sky is overcast, the rising sun barely visible.

A one-story house sits on a cramped lot. Chipped paint. Wilting bushes. The house might seem abandoned except that MICAH (black boy, 11) opens the front door and descends the steps alone.

His thin windbreaker puffs out from underneath the straps of his backpack. The bag is so heavy that he drags his feet as he turns up the sidewalk and continues down the road.

EXT. CITY STREET - DAY

The street is glum. The sidewalk is cracked. MICAH shuffles along beside a chain-link fence; he reaches his arm out to run his fingers across it and it RATTLES.

EXT. SCHOOLYARD - DAY

Behind the school, children of various ages scurry and play around a modest field, a playground, a basketball hoop mounted on a wall.

LAUGHTER as MICAH approaches the school. Young teenagers stand congregated by the corner of the building. Micah moves closer to watch the commotion.

At the center of the circle of students, IBRAHIM (brown boy, 14) beckons the crowd like a barker.

                    IBRAHIM
          Alright. Who next?

Ibrahim scans the crowd. Micah inches closer, timid, still behind the group. He catches glimpses of the action between the bodies in front of him.

                    IBRAHIM
          Come on. Don't be chickenshit.

A girl stands at the front of the crowd, arms crossed in a heavy bubblegoose. This is LATONYA (black girl, 14).

Ibrahim struts the circle. LaTonya catches his eye.

                    IBRAHIM
          You? You in?

She nods shyly.

                    LATONYA
          Yeah. Okay.

The CROWD HOOTS and cheers her on. Ibrahim leads her to the center of the circle.

                    IBRAHIM
          You ready?

                    LATONYA
          Explain it again.

                    IBRAHIM
          Okay. First you squat down and
          breathe real heavy. In and out. Like
          as heavy as you can. Twenty-five
          times. At least. Then stand up real
          fast, bite down on your thumb and
          blow out all the air you got.

                    LATONYA
          Then what?

                    IBRAHIM
          That's it.

                    LATONYA
          It's dangerous?

                    IBRAHIM
          Nah. It's like if you go underwater.
          Soon as your body needs air you just
          come back up.

LaTonya nods, smiles cautiously.

                    LATONYA
          Okay.

The crowd eggs her on. Ibrahim steps back.

                    IBRAHIM
          Go 'head.

LaTonya pauses, then pulls off her coat and tosses
it aside. She squats down, crosses her arms on her
chest, and starts heaving, sucking in and pushing
out quick, shallow breaths.

Micah's eyes are wide with wonder. Ibrahim smirks.

LaTonya hyperventilates for a few seconds before
springing to her feet. She bites down on her thumb
and blows out as hard as she can, exhaling.

Then her knees buckle underneath her.

Again the crowd erupts, GASPING AND LAUGHING.
LaTonya stays on the ground for a moment before
struggling back to her feet. She looks around,
dazed. Everyone watching clamors in amazement.

Ibrahim steps forward to pat the disoriented
girl on her back.

                    IBRAHIM
            You good, you good.

                    LATONYA
                  (confused)
            Yeah. I'm fine.

                    IBRAHIM
            Feels real good right?

LaTonya does not answer, but grabs haphazardly at
her coat and retakes her place in the crowd.

                    IBRAHIM
            Who next, who next?

                    MICAH (O.S.)
            Can I try?

The crowd falls silent. Everyone looks around.

Bodies part to reveal Micah. Ibrahim looks down on
him in disbelief.

                    IBRAHIM
            Word? You wanna get in on this?

Micah nods as Ibrahim steps closer.

                    IBRAHIM
            What you in? Like fourth grade?

                    MICAH
            Fifth.

CHUCKLES from the crowd; Micah bows his head.

                    IBRAHIM
           Nah, little guy. It's not for you.

Ibrahim reaches forward to shove Micah, a little
too hard.

                    IBRAHIM
           You should prolly just go comb your
           one pube.

Only the boys in the crowd laugh. Ibrahim steps
back as Micah slinks away.

                    IBRAHIM
           Come on. Somebody real get in here.

Micah lumbers to the front door of the school then
turns to look over the yard.

A group of girls jump double dutch. Some younger
kids run around, a game of tag. Another group of
kids obsesses over trading cards, pointing and
joking.

Micah is by himself.

He hears a DOG YAP and spins his head to see a
large golden retriever, big pleading eyes staring
up at him. This is WINNIE.

Micah rushes over to the dog, suddenly very
excited. He crouches down to pet her, rubs behind
her ears.

                    MICAH
           Winnie! You followed me all the way
           here?

The dog pants. Her tail wags incessantly.

                    MICAH
          Good girl... good girl.

Micah stops petting the dog as a SCHOOL BELL
RINGS. He frowns. The rest of the kids around the
schoolyard start to file into the building.

                    MICAH
                 (to Winnie)
          I gotta go.

Winnie stares blithely.

                    MICAH
          I'll see you after school. Then we
          can play, okay?

Micah rubs Winnie's head vigorously one last time
before standing up and retreating to the school
building.

                    MICAH
          Don't get hurt!

He turns and runs inside.

INT. CLASSROOM - DAY

The classroom is dreary. Inspirational posters
line the splotchy, lifeless walls.

   Is this poster a bad omen or a good sign?

   *Shoot for the moon. If you miss, probably it's
                dark at night.*

*Lord, grant me the serenity to separate church and
                    state.*

The posters do not inspire the students, who sit in silent rows of desks as the teacher, MS. LEVIN (white woman, mid 20s), drones on at the head of the classroom.

> MS. LEVIN
> So only after you make an observation, after you have a guess about what's going on... then you come up with an experiment.

Micah leans, head in hands, struggling to focus on the lecture. His eyes wander the room as Ms. Levin blathers.

> MS. LEVIN (O.S.)
> ...decide if what you're seeing is true or...

Nobody is paying attention. TILDEN (brown boy, 11) and UJANA (brown girl, 11) exchange furtive looks. Ujana scribbles something on a piece of paper, folds it up and passes it to Tilden. He blushes; she grins.

> MS. LEVIN (O.S.)
> ...test your hypothesis...

At the back of the room is a large window overlooking the schoolyard. As Micah's attention drifts to the outdoors, the expanse, the freedom, WINNIE pokes her head up at the bottom of the window.

> MS. LEVIN (O.S.)
> ...should be able to prove...

Micah notices the dog, watches with delight as she paws at the window, trying to maintain her balance, trying to see inside.

                   Micah? Micah. Micah!

Micah realizes he is being summoned and spins back
around to face the front of the room. His eyes
dart over the chalkboard, trying to figure out what
he missed.

                    MICAH
          Uh... sorry. Could you repeat the
          question?

                    MS. LEVIN
          How can you tell if your hypothesis
          is scientific?

                    MICAH
          If it's falsifiable. It has to be
          possible for the experiment to prove
          your idea wrong.

Ms. Levin glares; he's right and she doesn't like
it.

                    MS. LEVIN
          Please try to stay focused. I don't
          want you distracting anyone.

                    MICAH
               (sinking)
          Sorry.

Micah picks up his pencil and pretends to take
notes. Ms. Levin turns back to the chalkboard and
starts scrawling.

                    MS. LEVIN
          So when a theory gets proven false
          we have to replace it with one
          that...

As soon as he is sure his teacher won't notice, Micah turns back to the window. But Winnie has vanished.

INT. CAFETERIA - DAY

MICAH scowls. He stands in the doorway, over-looking the crowded lunchroom, brown paper bag clutched to his chest. He scans the cafeteria.

At one table, two students play paper football.

At another, a boy bangs A BEAT ON THE TABLE with his hands while his friends nod along.

At a third, TILDEN and UJANA sit across from each other, flirting the way fifth graders do: by pre-tending not to care about each other. They jabber and pick at their school lunches.

Micah watches them for a moment before stepping out of the doorway.

He nears the side of the table. Tilden and Ujana stop whispering to each other and look up at him.

> MICAH
> (nervous)
> Uh... hi.

> UJANA
> What?

> MICAH
> I'm Micah. I'm in your science class? With Ms. Levin?

> UJANA
> So?

                    MICAH
          Could I... sit here? And eat with
          you?

He looks back and forth between Tilden and Ujana.
They say nothing, a mix of disbelief and disgust
written on their faces.

                    MICAH
          If not, that's okay...

Tilden shakes his head.

                    TILDEN
          Sorry, man.

                    UJANA
          We're kind of having a
          conversation.

Micah bows his head.

                    MICAH
          Okay. Sorry.

He backs away from the table and walks off. Tilden
and Ujana turn back to each other, scoffing.

EXT. SCHOOLYARD - DAY

MICAH sits alone on a bench with his brown paper
lunch bag. He reaches into it and pulls out a
wrapped sandwich, little more than two slices of
white bread with a slab of bologna. He unwraps it
and takes a bite.

When he looks up, WINNIE is standing in front of
him, panting, tail wagging in anticipation.

Micah flashes a forlorn smile. He tears off a chunk of bologna and feeds it to her. She is grateful. Micah rubs her head.

                    MICAH
          Good girl.

INT. CLASSROOM - DAY

MICAH sits in agony at his desk, the room is silent. He watches impatiently. The clock's arms tick in an excruciatingly slow circle. It is 2:59.

And 57 seconds...

58...

59...

The SCHOOL BELL RINGS. Micah springs up out of his seat, grabs his backpack, and dashes for the door.

EXT. SCHOOLYARD - DAY

The doors of the schoolhouse burst open and a swarm of children spills out.

MICAH stops just past the threshold, still and surveying within the torrent of bodies.

It's hard to see anything in the chaos.

Then, through it, flashes of golden fur.

WINNIE weaves toward Micah against the current of the schoolkids' legs. She reaches the boy just as the crowd around him abates. He kneels to pet her and she bounces eagerly.

The sun falls low in the sky.

MICAH walks back up the same cracked sidewalk,
adorned again in his coat and backpack, much less
a burden now.

WINNIE gallops behind him. Micah reaches his arm
out and the FENCE RATTLES again. He turns around
and ambles backwards, goading Winnie into chasing
him. She bounds toward him.

EXT. MICAH'S HOUSE - NIGHT

MICAH traipses up the road, up the stairs, and
pulls open the door. WINNIE runs around in circles
in front of the house until MICAH WHISTLES at her.
She scampers into the house and Micah follows.

INT. HALLWAY (MICAH'S HOUSE) - NIGHT

MICAH drops his bag and hangs his coat on a hook.
WINNIE peers up at him attentively.

Down the hall his mother, TABITHA (black woman,
mid 30s), paces the kitchen. She doesn't notice
him come in.

INT. KITCHEN (MICAH'S HOUSE) - NIGHT

An empty can sits on the counter and a pot of soup
simmers on the stove.

TABITHA barely looks up as MICAH and WINNIE enter,
drooping with exhaustion. Slices of cheese shed
their plastic wrap and land on slices of bread.

Micah takes a seat at the table and hangs his
head. Winnie lies down on the floor next to him.

Silence.

Tabitha drops a sandwich onto a skillet. It
SIZZLES.

>   TABITHA
>   (facing the stove)
>   I'm making grilled cheese.

Micah says nothing.

>   TABITHA
>   (facing the stove)
>   You hungry?

>   MICAH
>   Kinda.

Silence again.

Tabitha stirs the soup.

>   TABITHA
>   (facing the stove)
>   Good day?

>   MICAH
>   Yeah. Okay.

>   TABITHA
>   (facing the stove)
>   What'd you do?

>   MICAH
>   Science. Language Arts. Social
>   Studies. Played with Winnie.

>   TABITHA
>   (facing the stove)
>   What?

                    MICAH
        She followed me to school.

                    TABITHA
                (facing the stove)
        Who's Winnie?

Micah pauses.

                    MICAH
        My dog.

                    TABITHA
                (facing the stove)
        You lobbying for a dog again?

                    MICAH
        What's "lobbying" mean?

                    TABITHA
                (facing the stove)
        I told you we can't afford it.

Micah looks down for Winnie. But the dog is gone.

                    TABITHA
                (gallows humor)
        I can barely feed you, sweetie.

Micah nods.

                    MICAH
        Sorry.

Tabitha flips the sandwich in the pan, then finally
turns to Micah with a sigh.

                    TABITHA
        Homework?

MICAH

Yeah.

TABITHA

Why don't you go get started? I'll
bring you food when it's ready.

Micah stands, wordless, and leaves the kitchen
alone.

INT. BEDROOM (MICAH'S HOUSE) - NIGHT

MICAH enters with his bulbous backpack, flicks on
the overhead light, and shuts the door behind him.

He tosses his backpack onto the twin bed pressed
against the wall. And he slumps down across from
it in a small wooden chair at a small wooden desk.
He stares blankly. A blank wall.

Behind him, WINNIE sits on the bed, curiously
translucent, but panting, watching intently. Micah
ignores her. She YIPS at him. He does not flinch.

He sits expressionless.

Then, slowly, he slides his chair backwards. The
LEGS SCRAPE against the floor. He steps to the
center of the room.

He crouches down, crosses his arms on his chest,
and takes a deep breath. Then another. Another.
With every breath, his respiration rate increases
until he is hyperventilating. He jumps to his
feet, bites down on his thumb, and blows all his
air out.

Winnie watches with sorrow as Micah's vision
blurs.

FADE TO:

Black.

The THUD OF A BODY COLLAPSING interrupted by the hard CRACK OF BONE.

Silence.

Then TABITHA calls from the kitchen.

                    TABITHA (O.S.)
          Hey what was that?
               (nothing)
          Micah?
               (nothing)
          Micah, you okay?

Another moment of silence.

                    TABITHA (O.S.)
          Micah?

TITLE CARD: THE FAINTING GAME

A DESERT OF DREAMING

SLO-MO (black person, any age) and DOUBLE-TIME
(black person, any age) sit on a bench, bored as
shit.

                    SLO-MO
          You read the news today?

                    DOUBLE-TIME
          Naw, why?

                    SLO-MO
          They caught that politician lying.

                    DOUBLE-TIME
          Aw shit. That same one from the
          thing?

                    SLO-MO
          Nah. The other one.

                    DOUBLE-TIME
          The one who had-

                    SLO-MO
          Yup! Caught him lying.

The two laugh heartily.

                    DOUBLE-TIME
          I knew he was lying! He din even
          look like he was telling the truth.

                    SLO-MO
          He really din!

Their rolling laughter slows to a chuckle, then a
sigh.

                    SLO-MO
          Lotta people died.

                    DOUBLE-TIME
          Yup.

A moment passes.

Then another.

The two look around, listless.

                    DOUBLE-TIME
          Ay you got a cigarette?

Slo-Mo pats their jacket down to check.

                    SLO-MO
          I don't even got any pockets.

                    DOUBLE-TIME
          Yes you do. Right there on your
          pants.

                    SLO-MO
          But I don't smoke.

                    DOUBLE-TIME
          Then why you aint just say no?

Slo-Mo shrugs.

Double-Time scowls, turns away to brood.

Boredom overtakes them and they turn back to Slo-
Mo.

                    DOUBLE-TIME
          It's none in that pocket?

Double-Time reaches across Slo-Mo's lap and in
doing so, turns their shoulders just enough to see
behind the bench.

                    SLO-MO
          Nah.

                    DOUBLE-TIME
          Hey... what's up with that guy?

                    SLO-MO
          What guy?

                    DOUBLE-TIME
          I been meaning to ask you.

                    SLO-MO
          Okay go.

                    DOUBLE-TIME
          Go where?

                    SLO-MO
          Ask me.

                    DOUBLE-TIME
          I did.

                    SLO-MO
          What?

                    DOUBLE-TIME
          What's up with that guy?

                    SLO-MO
          Who?

                    DOUBLE-TIME
          Him.

Double-Time turns to point behind the bench.

Behind them, an old man sits on a pole that juts up from a plot full of rubble, worn-down bricks, and eroded boards. The man wears a depression-era suit, a sharp hat, and a long white beard. This is MONON (black person, old as fuck).

Monon's eyes loll with either disinterest or delirium. He smiles and nods and licks his teeth.

                    SLO-MO
          I don't think he smokes either.

                    DOUBLE-TIME
          But I'm saying. Who is he?

                    SLO-MO
          Oh that's Monon, Who Keeps the
          Desert of Dreaming.

                    DOUBLE-TIME
          Monon?

Slo-Mo nods.

                    SLO-MO
          Yeah. Who Keeps the Desert of
          Dreaming.

Double-Time turns back to look at the man.

Monon digs into his beard to scratch his chin.

Double-Time looks skeptical.

                    DOUBLE-TIME
          So he just sits there?

                    SLO-MO
          His house collapsed and he was too
          old to move so he din. He been
          sitting there forever.

                    DOUBLE-TIME
          Forever?

                    SLO-MO
          Least since I moved here.

                    DOUBLE-TIME
          When was that?

                    SLO-MO
          Hm. I don't remember.

Double-Time nods.

                    DOUBLE-TIME
          Maybe I'll go buy a cigarette.

                    SLO-MO
          Just one?

                    DOUBLE-TIME
          It's no cigarette guy round here?

                    SLO-MO
          I think they killed him.

                    DOUBLE-TIME
          Damn.

A solemn moment of silence.

                    DOUBLE-TIME
          I don't got enough for a whole pack.

Double-Time stews angrily.

But they get over it.

                    DOUBLE-TIME
          How does Monon buy food?

                    SLO-MO
          Who Keeps the Desert of Dreaming?

                    DOUBLE-TIME
          Yeah. What does he eat?

                    SLO-MO
          He don't need to eat. He's fed by
          the sun.

Double-Time shakes his head.

                    DOUBLE-TIME
          That don't make no sense.

They think.

                    DOUBLE-TIME
          Somebody must be sneaking him food.

Slo-Mo shrugs.

                    SLO-MO
          They aint catch nobody.

                    DOUBLE-TIME
          Just a matter of time.

                    SLO-MO
          I guess.

Double-Time digs around in their pockets.

Nothing in the first one.

But from the second, they produce a small flask.

Excited, they tip it back to take a swig.

Nothing.

> DOUBLE-TIME
> Empty.

Slo-Mo droops idly.

Double-Time upends the flask, desperate for a drop.

They screw the cap back on and jam the flask back into their pocket.

It disappears.

> DOUBLE-TIME
> (annoyed)
> What does he even want anyway?

Slo-Mo looks up to Double-Time, inquisitive, waiting.

> DOUBLE-TIME
> (relenting)
> Monan, Who Keeps the Desert of Dreaming.

> SLO-MO
> We should go talk to him.

> DOUBLE-TIME
> Why?

> SLO-MO
> He might be interesting.

                    DOUBLE-TIME
          How? He sits in the same spot all
          day.

Double-Time stretches their legs out.

                    DOUBLE-TIME
          I don't know how you could do that.

                    SLO-MO
          He's happy.

                    DOUBLE-TIME
          He prob'ly senile.

                    SLO-MO
          Senile people get happy too, I bet.

                    DOUBLE-TIME
          Why you on his side?

Double-Time shifts anxiously.

                    DOUBLE-TIME
          I wish I had a cigarette.

                    SLO-MO
          That make you happy?

Double-Time thinks it through.

TITLE CARD: A DESERT OF DREAMING

'TIL I GET BACK

INT. BASEMENT - NIGHT.

Black.

A VOICE cuts through.

> VOICE (O.S.)
> Tell me a joke.

SYX (black trans woman, late 20s), smooth-faced in a floral-print dress, hair pulled back into two afro puffs, nestled awkwardly against the arm of the sofa. Garishly dressed for a night out, AMANDA (white woman, late 20s) waves at the couch from a recliner. The PARTY BUSTLES around them.

> AMANDA (VOICE)
> Come on. You must know one.

GULL (black woman, late 20s) and Syx shift awkwardly, cornered on the couch. Gull, a bit more masculine than Syx, rises with a beer bottle.

> GULL
>
> Aiight, I got one. There's this
> guy — call him Jack — and he's
> angry with the world because no one
> likes him and he has no friends.

Amanda's eyes are on her phone.

> AMANDA
> Relatable.

> GULL
> So he decides he's gonna rob a bank.

Amanda looks up.

                    AMANDA
          Mmm... maybe not.

                    GULL
          He goes out and buys a gun and runs
          up in a bank and takes like a
          hundred people hostage. But one of
          the tellers presses the silent alarm
          and a SWAT team shows up.

Gull pantomimes setting up tripod guns. Amanda is
suddenly rapt.

                    GULL
          So the negotiator calls into the
          bank like, "Hello Jack. I'm a
          negotiator and it's my job to make sure
          this all works out so that no
          one gets hurt. You want that too,
          right?" And Jack's just panicking
          like, "Yeah."

Syx watches curiously.

                    GULL
          So the negotiator goes, "Great. Then
          we're on the same side. I think I
          can help you, Jack. I want us to be
          friends." And Jack breaks down.

Gull exaggerates, crying.

                    GULL
          "A friend is all I ever wanted..."

She locks eyes with Syx.

                    GULL
          "...I just needed someone to care
          about me."

Syx blushes.

                    GULL
          So the negotiator says, "Why don't
          you come out here? We can talk about
          it." And Jack gets quiet. "The whole
          place is surrounded with cops
          right?"

Amanda, eyes wide, leans in.

Gull, the negotiator, nods.

                    GULL
          "Yup." So Jack says, "You think
          they'll watch-"

She freezes as THE BOOGA interrupts.

                    THE BOOGA (V.O.)
          It's farther than that.

Static.

INT. BEDROOM - DAY

A chubby, smiling INFANT (black child, around 1)
squirms on their back on a lumpy twin bed. SYX
speaks.

                    SYX (O.S.)
               (nervous)
          Who came?

Now donning close-cropped hair, a little cheek
stubble, and an ill-fitting suit, Syx turns
nervously back to GULL for an answer. Gull tugs
inconspicuously at the corset under her ruffled
dress.

                    GULL
          Jesse, Mack, and Julie.

                    SYX
          Thassit?

                    GULL
          Gotta start someplace.

                    SYX
          If we're gonna run this place on
          our-

                    GULL
          Ay.

                    SYX
          I just mean if our debt-

                    GULL
          Ay. We'll get there.

Gull lays a reassuring hand on Syx's arm; Syx nods
and sighs. The three breathe deeply.

A SHOTGUN BLAST sounds from outside the room; Gull
and Syx snap to attention and rush to the door.

A SECOND GUNSHOT.

INT. HALLWAY - DAY (CONTINUOUS)

SYX and GULL hurry down the hall toward the back door. As they arrive at the door, a THIRD SHOTGUN BLAST rings out. Through the transom, they see MACK (black man, late 20s) fall to the ground.

EXT. YARD - DAY (CONTINUOUS)

A WHITE MAN (white man, late 20s) with a shotgun looms over MACK, who is still twitching and sputtering.

                    WHITE MAN
          It aint yours, y'hear? Y'aint taking
          my land and y'aint getting a penny
          more in pay. You work for me.

INT. HALLWAY - DAY (CONTINUOUS)

GULL's mouth hangs open. She reaches impulsively for the doorknob, but SYX grabs her wrist to stop her.

The BABY SQUEALS.

Syx starts to backpedal down the hall.

They freeze. THE BOOGA.

                    THE BOOGA (V.O.)
          No! Back more. Way back.

Static.

INT. HOVEL - NIGHT

A splash of water hits a long, thin gash on a calf. SYX winces. Their arms and legs are covered in lash scars, jutting from underneath their loose linen clothing.

The flesh of their leg is freshly split; GULL
reaches an arm out, itself streaked with scars, to
examine Syx's leg.

> GULL
> Luck this all you got.

> SYX
> (wincing)
> Dun feel like luck.

> GULL
> Do to your grandkid.

Gull wraps a thin blanket tightly around the
wound. This leaves the two with nothing to lie on,
so they lean against a wall.

Syx hangs their head in silent contemplation.

> SYX
> Think we gon see the harvest this
> year?

> GULL
> I reckon.

Syx winces again.

> SYX
> Why?

> GULL
> Cuz if not the farm don't run.

> SYX
> Maybe easier to just run in the
> water.

Gull motions at the makeshift bandage wrapped
around Syx's leg.

                    GULL
          You running away with that?

                    SYX
          Not away. Just in. I think about it.
          Sometimes. More'n more.

Gull considers but shakes her head.

                    GULL
          You can't.

                    SYX
          You say I have to stay.

                    GULL
          No.

                    SYX
          Forever.

                    GULL
No. We don't gotta stay. If you say
run we run.

Syx turns their head away, but Gull reaches out to
their cheek, pulls their focus gently back to the
conversation.

                    GULL
          This...

She lays a hand on Syx's leg; Syx swats it away.

                    SYX
          Ow!

                    GULL
          Flesh is—

Static.

Bright white lights break through the image. SYX
writhes.

INT. HOVEL - NIGHT

GULL hasn't noticed.

                    GULL
          —need the flesh—

Static.

INT. PADDED ROOM - DAY

SYX strapped to a chair, disoriented, dizzy,
squirming against their restraints. Their eyes
struggle to focus.

Across the room, two white men in an argument. One
man, the TECHNICIAN (white man, late 20s) wears a
white lab coat, twists knobs on an arcane machine.
The other, in a bulletproof vest but no sleeves,
berates him; this is THE BOOGA (white man, mid
30s).

The Booga stomps back over to Syx and leans down,
uncomfortably close to their face.

                    THE BOOGA
          Listen to me, Six. Your ancestors
          gave you the key to survival.
          Whatever black magic crystal spell
          bullshit you got in your head, we
          need it. Now. It's our time to
          survive. We're going to send you
          back again. And the next time we
          talk you better have some answers.

Static.

INT. BEDROOM - DAY

SYX, with a suit and stubble, holds the INFANT
tightly in their arms, solemn, rocking the child.
GULL steps into the doorframe.

Syx cannot manage a smile.

                    GULL (V.O.)
          Flesh...

Neither can Gull.

                    GULL (V.O.)
          Flesh is part of you but not all.

Syx's eyes well with water as they rub the
infant's back.

                    GULL (V.O.)
          You need the flesh to run.

                    SYX
          Shh, shh, shh.

INT. HOVEL - NIGHT

GULL, still pleading with SYX.

                    GULL
          And fight, too. But people aint just
          flesh. Is you people?

                    SYX
          Yeah.

                    GULL
          Then somebody gave you life. And you
          give life to somebody else.

> SYX
>
> You with chile?

Gull smirks.

> GULL
>
> Not yet.

She leans her head on Syx's shoulder.

INT. BASEMENT - NIGHT

GULL drops triumphantly back into her seat on the sofa. AMANDA, annoyed.

> AMANDA
>
> What? That's stupid.

SYX snickers, cheeks almost as high as their afro puffs.

> SYX
>
> I liked it.

> AMANDA
>
> It didn't make any sense.

SOME WHITE GUY (white man, around 30) and SOME OTHER WHITE GUY (white man, around 30) arrive by Amanda's side around the recliner. She confers with them for a second, nodding in hushed tones.

> AMANDA
>
> Alright I'm coming with you then.

She motions toward Gull and Syx on the couch.

> AMANDA
> (to Some White Guy)
> Watch them.

And she walks off with Some Other White Guy.
Syx and Gull blink, stupefied.

INT. HOVEL - DAY

Huddled to SYX's shoulder, GULL curls a hand
around their arm.

                    GULL
You can't just disappear into the
water. Gotta give them kin a chance
to thank you.

Static.

INT. PADDED ROOM - DAY

SYX twists, eyes rolled back in their sockets,
wrists red against the belts holding them to the
chair.

THE BOOGA yells at the TECHNICIAN.

                    THE BOOGA
          Well what's taking so long?

Syx rasps.

                    SYX
          We don't have to do this.

The Booga turns to face them.

                    THE BOOGA
          What you sayda me?

Syx lifts their head to meet The Booga's eye.

                    SYX
          We don't have to do this. If you
          want the secret, all you have to do
          is ask.

                  THE BOOGA
               (a threat)
          Okay. Then what is it?

Static.

INT. LOFT - DAY

SYX lies on their back, staring at the ceiling,
earbuds in, nodding to the beat. GULL pokes their
head over the side of the loft bed. Syx pulls one
earbud out.

                    GULL
          I made breakfast.

Syx smiles.

EXT. GARDEN - DAY

SYX and GULL, each in a long, flowing robe, sit
across the table from one another. Gull reaches
over her finished breakfast plate to move a piece
on a hexagonal chess board. She leans back to
watch Syx, who in turn leans forward to examine
the new state of the board.

                    GULL
          So what were you thinking about in
          there?

Syx squints harder.

                         SYX
                    (deflecting)
                  Just reminiscing.

                         GULL
              You seemed lost in thought.

Syx breaks focus to eye Gull suspiciously.

                         SYX
              You tryna distract me?

                         GULL
                  Is it working?

Syx moves a piece smugly.

                         SYX
                  No.

Gull looks down at the board.

                         GULL
                  You sure?

She moves a piece.

                         GULL
                  Mate.

She gets up, gathers the plates, pecks an annoyed
Syx on the cheek, then absconds into the house.

Static.

INT. PADDED ROOM - DAY

SYX, with an unnervingly knowing smile. THE BOOGA
is impatient.

                    THE BOOGA
        Well?

                    SYX
        Secret is I don't need magic. I got
        me.

With one final, exerted jerk, Syx breaks from the
wrist restraints and lunges for The Booga's neck.

                                        CUT TO:

TITLE CARD: 'TIL I GET BACK

ACKNOWLEDGEMENTS

1. *Handstyle* was a semifinalist in the 2017 Hollywood Just4Shorts Film and Screenplay Competition.

2. *Shyla* was selected as the overall winner of the 2018 BOLT by Barnstorm screenplay competition. It was produced and the resulting film premiered at the 2019 Roxbury International Film Festival.

3. *The Fainting Game* was selected by the 2020 SUNYWide Film Festival and was a quarterfinalist in The Film Empire's Diversity Mentorship for Screenwriters competition.

BIOGRAPHY

Marshall "gripp" Gillson is a writer / programmer / educator based primarily on the internet. Marshall graduated from Morehouse College in 2009 and the Georgia Institute of Technology in 2012. Their work is multimedia and interdisciplinary, ranging from written word to performance art to electronic installation. They have appeared onstage as an actor and a poet, self-published and been printed in literary magazines, built digital chapbooks and Twitter bots, taught college courses and workshops, and have written, produced, and appeared in short films.

Marshall's television pilot Offbeat / But On Point won the 2020 Table Read My Screenplay competition and was produced and broadcast as a table read. In 2019, Marshall co-wrote and -produced the grant-funded stageplay SPIRIT, which premiered to a three-show run in October. Marshall was recognized by the 2019 Roxbury International Film Festival with the Kay Bourne Emerging Filmmaker award after their short film Shyla premiered at the festival. Marshall debuted the role of Nathanael Grene in AS220s 2017 production of A Furtive Movement: the Use of Farce. Marshall is also a nationally acclaimed spoken word performer and appeared on the National Poetry Slam final stage twice in adjacent years.

Much of Marshall's work is fantastical, surreal, and absurdist. It confronts race, gender, mental imbalance, loneliness, existential dread, and sometimes robots. In their spare time, they enjoy board games, avoiding attention, and writing biographies in the third person.